D1498272

A ROUNDABOUT TURN

OTHER BOOKS
with drawings by
LESLIE BROOKE

JOHNNY CROW'S GARDEN

JOHNNY CROW'S PARTY

JOHNNY CROW'S NEW GARDEN

THE GOLDEN GOOSE BOOK
The Three Little Pigs
Tom Thumb
The Golden Goose
The Three Bears

RING O' ROSES
Oranges and Lemons
The Man in the Moon
Little Bo-Peep
This Little Pig went to Market

LESLIE BROOKE'S LITTLE BOOKS
Size 7 ins. by 5½ ins.
4 Books—Nursery Stories
4 Books—Nursery Rhymes

THE HOUSE IN THE WOOD

THE NURSERY RHYME BOOK
Edited by Andrew Lang

Published by
FREDERICK WARNE & CO. LTD

A ROUNDABOUT TURN

BY

ROBERT H·CHARLES

WITH DRAWINGS BY

L·LESLIE BROOKE

DENVER
PUBLIC LIBRARY
973
COUNTY OF DENVER

LONDON

FREDERICK WARNE & CO·LTD·

& NEW YORK

G399431

RO1000 21170

THESE VERSES APPEARED ORIGINALLY IN *PUNCH*, AND THE
AUTHOR'S THANKS ARE DUE TO ITS PROPRIETORS
FOR THEIR KIND PERMISSION TO
PRINT THEM HERE.

COPYRIGHT IN ALL COUNTRIES
SIGNATORY TO THE BERNE CONVENTION
FREDERICK WARNE & CO. LTD.
LONDON
ENGLAND
Printed in Great Britain

JE

A ROUNDABOUT TURN.

A TOAD that lived on Albury Heath
Wanted to see the World.

" It isn't that I dislike the Heath,
" It's a perfectly charming Heath, of course—

" All this heather, and all this gorse,
" All this bracken to walk beneath,
" With its feathery fronds to the sky uncurled—
" It's as jolly a Heath as ever was found,

" But it's flat, and the World, they say, is round.
" Yes, fancy," he said, " it's round, they tell me.
" And wouldn't I like to go and see !

" But there—it's a long way down the road
" For a fellow that walks as slow as a Toad.

" If I had a horse, I'd go," said he,
" If only I had a horse !
" Who's got a horse," he cried, " to sell me ? "

Well, nobody had, you see.

BUT horses came to the Heath one day,
Mettlesome steeds in brave array,
With prancing legs and staring eyes,
And crimson saddles that fall and rise
As round the galloping squadron flies,
And tents, and swings, and cokernut shies,
And a hoop-la stall with many a prize,
And races, and a band, and cheering.

" Hark ! " said the Toad, " what's this I'm hearing ?
" It must be the World arrived, by the sound ;
" *Now* I'll see if it's really round ! "

OFF he crawled to the thick of things,
   And the crowds made crawling rather tiring.
"Dear me," he said, "I wish I'd wings!
"If this is the World," said he, perspiring,

" It's inconveniently full of Feet."

When a sudden voice said, " Look—how sweet !
" Mummy, a toad ! Let's give him a treat.

" It's not very safe for him on the ground,
" So I'll put him up——

——on the merry-go-round."

AND before the Toad could answer the floor began to
slide,
The horses started prancing, and the riders settled to ride,
And they all moved faster, and the band began to play,
And away round he went with them, away and away and
away.
Hooray ! . . . .

DENVER
PUBLIC LIBRARY
NOV 1973
CITY & COUNTY OF DENVER

SO the Toad rode the Roundabout
    Round and round and round;
No one minded him, he sat without a sound:
He rather liked the movement, he rather liked the tune,
    He just rode the Roundabout
All the afternoon.

WHEN the time to pay came
        What did he do?
" Tuppence a ride! Tuppence a ride! How much for
    you? "
Some had ridden for one ride, some had ridden for two—
    " *Seventy-nine*," the Toad cried ;
The Boy said, " Coo ! "

" But never you mind," the Toad replied.
" Here's an I.O.U."

" AND now," he said, " I'll go, thanks,
"I want to get home to tea.

" Another for nothing ? *No*, thanks,
" *Not* any more for me."

HOME, holding the grasses,
Crawling a crooked road,

Slowly there passes

A very unsteady

Toad.

"WELL, and what have you found, dear?
    " And what have you seen and heard?

" Is the World really round, dear ? "
  " *Round ?* " he said. " My word !
" *Round ?* " said he ; " you should feel it spin !
" Roundest place I ever was in !—
  " Round ! " he chuckled ; " it's that !
" But it's rather," he said with a knowing wink—
" It's rather a *giddy* place, I think.

" Give me a drop of the dew to drink,
" And give me the Heath ;

  it's flat ! "

PRINTED IN GREAT BRITAIN FOR THE PUBLISHERS
BY WILLIAM CLOWES AND SONS LTD
LONDON AND BECCLES
1443.1065